ELLA'S TRIP to ISRAEL

Vivian Newman

illustrated by
Akemi Gutierrez

KAR-BEN
PUBLISHING

To Becca, Jonah, and Micah, and the many wonderful summers that we spent exploring Israel together – V.N.

For Connor, Kelsey, and Kerry Keegan – A.G.

KAR-BEN Publishing
A division of Lerner Publishing Group, Inc.
241 First Avenue North
Minneapolis, MN 55401 U.S.A.
800-4KARBEN

Website address: www.karben.com

Library of Congress Cataloging-in-Publication Data

Newman, Vivian.
Ella's trip to Israel / by Vivian Newman ; illustrated by Akemi Guttierez.
p. cm.
Summary: A young girl travels through Israel with her parents and best friend Koofi, a stuffed monkey, whose misadventures are never a problem.
ISBN 978–0–7613–6029–2 (pbk. : alk. paper)
[1. Voyages and travels—Fiction. 2. Toys—Fiction. 3. Jews—Fiction. 4. Israel—Fiction.] I. Guttierez, Akemi, ill. II. Title.
PZ7.N4864Ell 2011
[E]—dc22 2009043785

Manufactured in the United States of America
2 – PC – 11/1/11

Ella is very excited. She and her family are going on a trip to Israel. Ella is traveling with her mom, her dad, and her good friend, Koofi the Kof. "Kof" is the Hebrew word for "monkey."

The airplane ride is very long. Ella watches a movie, reads books, eats a meal, and drinks lots and lots of mango juice.

Ella loves the juice. She has never tasted mango juice before. Koofi loves the juice, too, but it makes his fur very wet and sticky.

"*Eyn ba'aya*. **No problem,"**
says the Israeli flight attendant.

The Kotel in Jerusalem is the family's first stop. Many people pray at this wall which was once part of the ancient Temple.

Ella sees visitors writing notes on little slips of paper and putting them into cracks in the wall. Her mom tells her they are wishes and thank you's.

Ella wants to do this, too. Her mom helps her write her note.

As they fold the note, a little boy says *"Shalom"* to Koofi and tugs hard on his tail.

***"Eyn ba'aya.*
No problem,"
says Ella's mom.

In Tel Aviv, Ella and Koofi say "ooh" and "aah" as they look up at the many tall and interesting buildings.

At the outdoor market, Ella and her family stop to buy some food for lunch. Ella loves felafel. Koofi loves felafel too, but he wishes that the *tahini* was not so drippy.

"*Eyn ba'aya.* **No problem,"**
says Ella's dad.

At the Dead Sea, Ella and her mom and dad cover themselves with mud. Ella's mom tells her that the Dead Sea mud is very good for skin. Ella laughs. How funny they look! Koofi covers himself with mud, too.

Oops! The mud won't wash off Koofi's fur as easily as it rinses off Ella's skin.

"*Eyn ba'aya.* No problem,"
says Ella's mom.

Ella and her family travel north to the Galil, where they visit a kibbutz. Ella enjoys helping with the farm work on the kibbutz. She picks and eats grapes and dates.

Best of all, Ella helps milk the cows. "Plink, plink, plink," sings the milk as it hits the bottom of Ella's pail. "Swishhh," sounds the milk as it squirts into Koofi's face and eyes.

"*Eyn ba'aya.* **No problem,**" says the kibbutznik who is in charge of the cows and the dairy.

Ella's trip to Israel is over. Ella and Koofi love looking at the photo album with all the pictures from their trip.

"Koofi," says Ella's mom. "Your fur is like a photo album, too. All we have to do is look at you, and we can remember our whole trip!"

"*Eyn ba'aya.*
**No problem,
Koofi,"** whispers Ella.
"I love you just
the way you are."